WAKE UP TO A NEW KIND OF TERROR—an electrifying chase through the concrete labyrinth of a steam-tunnel system, where *something* lurks in the shadows.

Something big.

Something hungry ...

It's blood sport for the crazies who organize these nocturnal hunts, and a game of death for their latest victim. But unlike all the others, he's a man well acquainted with death. A man who has murdered for money. A man who intends to kill the thing that's stalking him—and kill it hard.

DIE WIDE AWAKE is a 20,000 word novella from the *New York Times* and *USA Today* bestselling author of *Cold Around the Heart* and *Skin in the Game*.

DIE WIDE AWAKE

Also by Michael Prescott

Manstopper

Kane

Shiver

Shudder

Shatter

Deadly Pursuit

Blind Pursuit

Mortal Pursuit

Comes the Dark

Stealing Faces

The Shadow Hunter

Last Breath

Next Victim

In Dark Places

Dangerous Games

Mortal Faults

Final Sins

Riptide

Grave of Angels

Cold Around the Heart

Steel Trap & Other Stories

Chasing Omega

Blood in the Water

Bad to the Bone

Skin in the Game

The Street

DIE WIDE AWAKE

MICHAEL PRESCOTT

Die Wide Awake
by Michael Prescott
Copyright © 2017 Douglas Borton
All rights reserved.

ISBN-13: 978-1981368716
ISBN-10: 198136871X

1

"Hey, you. Sir Galahad."

Slowly I climb up out of bad dreams and open my eyes. I'm in an alley in the dark, with soft rodent rustlings all around and two men standing over me.

They're lean and wiry, with matching suits and matching faces, narrow and angular, their black hair slicked back. They have to be brothers. The suits are expensive, Armani or something like it, with open-collared shirts. I've never approved of wearing a suit without a tie, and I don't approve of these two.

Also, they're young, less than half my age, a fact that annoys me on general principles.

The one closest to me, taller and evidently the older of the two, smiles down on me. Smiles too hard, like a salesman intent on closing a deal.

"So, my man," he says as if continuing a friendly talk, "how'd you like to make some money?"

Some questions should automatically put anyone on high alert. This is one of them.

I hike myself up to a sitting position against the brick wall and wrap the oilskin duster a little tighter around my body.

"Doing what?" I ask.

The words come out throaty and raw. It's been a long time since I've spoken. In the alley my only companions are rats and black beetles, and none of them are too interested in conversation.

"See that young lady there?" He points to a slice of urban street framed between the alley walls. A black BMW convertible sits at the curb, the top down, a girl of about twenty in the backseat. She has red hair. Bright red, flaming. Even in the rancid monochrome glow of mercury vapor streetlights, I can tell.

She stares in my direction, and I stare back.

"What about her?"

"We want you to fuck her."

I refocus my gaze on the joker in front of me. "You want me to fuck her," I say, repeating the words just to taste their strangeness.

"That's right. You fuck her, we watch. There's two hundred bucks in it for you."

I look at the younger brother, who nods reassuringly.

"Now why," I say slowly, "would you want me to do that?"

"It's what we're into, that's all. Her, too. She likes it. She's got a thing for the down and out."

"No offense." That's the other one, speaking for the first time.

They're just boys. College age. Their features are foreign—Middle Eastern, I think. No accents, though. They were brought up in this country. They have money, and they're slumming. A couple of bon vivants out on the town in their thousand-dollar suits and their hundred-thousand-dollar car.

The two of them are grinning at me. To them I'm an object of amusement. I don't mind that. It's better than being an object of pity.

"Where is this supposed to happen?" I ask.

"Motel. We know a place. Used it before."

I give the matter serious thought, looking it over from a variety of angles. The offer does not offend me or violate my moral sensibilities. I have no moral sensibilities. Still, it doesn't add up.

"Why don't you just fuck her yourselves?" I ask finally.

"I told you, we're into this kind of deal."

"We like to watch," the younger one adds.

"And she likes it when we watch. We may even video it. You could end up on YouTube. You could be a star."

"It's a whole thing," his brother says.

"Sure. You know. Everybody's got their thing."

I nod. This is true. Everybody does indeed have their thing. Even so, I am tolerably certain the brothers are lying.

"YouTube," I say, simply to buy time. "My fifteen minutes of fame."

"That's right. Like Marshall McLuhan said. But you've never heard of him."

"I've heard of him. But it was Andy Warhol."

"Oh, yeah. The spatter-art guy."

"Campbell's Soup cans. Pop art. Jackson Pollock was spatter."

"No shit. Did you used to be a professor or something?"

"Or something."

"How'd you hit rock bottom?"

"Does it matter?"

The kid shrugs. "Curiosity. I'm a people person."

That's another lie. He doesn't give a damn about me. Which is fair enough, because I don't give a damn about him.

The girl, though ...

"So," the older one says, "you in or out, Hobo Joe?"

I look toward the car again. The girl's eyes are wide and bright, but not with excitement. With fear, possibly. Yes.

It could be fear.

"Yo, we're on a schedule here. Offer's on the table. Take it or leave it."

His brother giggles. "I think this ragpicker's brain-dead. Dementia or some fucking thing. Nothing between the ears."

"That it, Trash Can Man? You senile?"

I ignore them. I'm still thinking about those eyes.

I've seen eyes like those before. Frightened. Helpless.

Another girl's eyes.

"Fuck it." The older one has lost patience. "You don't want us to pimp you out, we'll find another lucky winner. Shame, though. Our girl showed a definite interest, though I can't imagine what she sees in a gnawed old bone like you."

They're turning away when I say, "I'm in."

He makes a show of looking annoyed. "Took your sweet time deciding. What if we don't want you anymore?"

I never answer hypotheticals.

When I get to my feet, I put a little more effort

into it than necessary. These two already see me as old and busted, and I see no point in having them think otherwise. I've lost a lot of weight in recent years, and the long riding coat, which has been with me throughout my vagabond odyssey, hangs too loosely on my frame.

"Shit, this zombie's got a stink on him," the younger brother says. "Could be the worst one yet."

Interesting choice of words. I wonder how many others there have been, and where they are now.

"All right." The taller one claps me on the back, an affable gesture curiously devoid of friendliness. "Let's get a move on, Beau Brummel."

I give him props for the reference. Not many members of his generation would know it.

"And bring your stuff with you," he adds.

"I don't have any stuff."

"Even better."

I walk out of the alley, coat flaps beating at my ankles, in the company of my new friends.

This is how it starts.

2

WE BLOW OUT OF town on the turnpike with the top down and the wind beating at us with its fists. The girl and I are jammed together in the backseat. I try to meet her eyes, but she looks steadily away, clutching her purse tight against her breasts. I ought to talk to her, but it's been a long time since I initiated a conversation.

It's not as if I took a vow of silence or anything. It's just that I've lost the habit of speech, or of sleeping indoors, or of being a civilized man.

Though in truth, I'm not sure I ever was one of those.

The brothers, bookended up front, keep nodding their heads and laughing. Whatever they're up to, they've done it before, possibly many times. If they haven't been stopped by now, it's only because they're lucky, as bad people so often are.

I know about that. I'm one of the bad people, and I was uncommonly lucky for too many years.

Though I do my best to eavesdrop, the wind and the throb of hip-hop from the dashboard steal most of their words. The only one I can catch sounds like "Draco," which, if I remember correctly, is a constellation visible in far northern latitudes. I figure I must have heard wrong. These two don't strike me as astronomy buffs.

I have a fix on the brothers by now. Remember Saddam Hussein's boys, Uday and Qusay? They were rumored to be even crazier and more sadistic than their old man. One of them had his own bodyguard beaten to death because the poor son of a bitch happened to catch the eye of a girl the Hussein boy liked.

I don't know if this pair is Iraqi or Iranian or whatever, but by the looks of them, they have roots in that part of the world, they have a rich papa who's clearly been lax about laying down the law, and they're total shits. That makes them Uday and Qusay in my book.

As I recall, Uday was the older brother, so I name the talkative one after him. His silent partner is Qusay.

I like having names for people. If I don't know someone's real name, I make one up. It gives me a sense of control—of possession, almost. You know how the first thing you do when you get a pet is come up with a name for it? It's how you assert ownership.

So there they are: Uday and Qusay, young and stupid, looking for trouble. And finding me.

We speed on, deep into the rural heart of the state. This motel of theirs is apparently a lot farther off than I assumed.

The drive gives me plenty of time to think. One thing I'm sure of is that there's not going to be any sex show. The cover story is bullshit. The likelihood of foul play seems high, especially since I've already made out an armpit holster printing under

Uday's jacket. Qusay wears a looser suit, but he's probably carrying, as well.

Guns don't faze me. What matters isn't the weapon but the man wielding it. These two probably see themselves as tough guys, but by comparison with some of the people I've known, they're as dangerous as blind puppies.

As for me, I don't carry a gun anymore. But I can still make somebody dead.

It's not my fight, of course. I could've told the dynamic duo to fuck off. But there's the girl squeezed in beside me. She doesn't resemble Rebecca in any obvious way. Even so, she's about the right age. And she's in bad company, as Rebecca once was.

Redemption? Salvation? Is that the game plan?

I don't think so. I'm not the sentimental type. My world is a hard place made of sharp edges, and softness of any kind has no place in it. And I know I can't make things right. My past is set, and my future ... I have no future. I barely have a present. Half the time I think I'm already dead. I'm the ghost of a man.

Still, I can do the right thing, just once. I can play the hero, rescue the maiden in distress.

Uday did call me Sir Galahad, after all.

3

IT TAKES US MORE than an hour to get where we're going, which turns out to be a sad little run of closed-down strip malls and low-income housing choked off by pine woods. At the edge of town run miles of perimeter fencing, behind which lie the blocky shapes of shuttered buildings. From their uniformity and stark functionality, I peg them as military housing. The place is a fort, or it was. Two buildings, widely separated, show lights in the windows. The rest are dark and still, like dead things.

Uday turns onto the main access road and approaches the gatehouse, where a drowsy guard lolls, TV flicker reflected in his glasses. When he sees the BMW pull up, he snaps alert. And like the girl, he looks scared.

"Evening, guys," he says with false joviality. I notice he's not looking at them. Afraid to meet their eyes. "Didn't expect you tonight."

"When do you ever expect us?" Uday asks in a vaguely challenging way.

"I don't. I mean, never. I mean, it's none of my business when you come and go."

Babbling. He's soft-featured, milky-eyed, well into his sixties. Some of these security drones are ex-cops, but he's not. More like the proprietor of a mom-and-pop store that went under and took his life savings with it, obliging him to seek whatever employment he could find.

"The place quiet?" Uday asks.

"Hardly anyone around. Couple people working late in the brokerage firm, that's all."

Uday nods. "Well, you going to let us in or not?"

"Of course, sir. Of course." The gate lifts, and the BMW breezes through. I glance back and see the guard staring after us, his face a shrinking white oval in his glass booth.

I thought I had a handle on what was going on, but the fort obliges me to reconsider. The woods would be the right place for the sort of action I anticipated. But maybe Uday and Qusay aren't the outdoor type. Maybe they don't want to get any mud on their expensive Italian shoes.

See, the way I figure it, they're on a hobo hunt. They're people who take *The Most Dangerous Game* a little too seriously, and they've sized me up as a passable stand-in for Joel McCrea. Snatch a homeless guy, set him loose in the woods, hunt him down. Well, the woods are out, but a nearly deserted fort with a lone security guard on the take may serve equally well.

The girl's role in it is something I can't fathom. But I expect it will all become clear soon enough.

We motor down the main drive, past the black hulks of vacant buildings. The hip-hop has been silenced, making conversation possible. Uday takes advantage of the opportunity to play tour guide.

"This was an Army base," he explains. "Shut down ten years ago. The local rubes are trying to reinvent it as an industrial park. So far there's only a couple of businesses. It's mostly empty. But the power plant is operational. The two companies that moved in need heat, AC, and running water."

His interest in the HVAC and plumbing systems is puzzling, but I ask no questions.

The BMW hooks down a side street and parks outside a seemingly random building, an unlit, abandoned pile identical to all the others.

"This is our stop," Uday announces. "Everybody out."

The occupants in front disembark first, allowing those of us sardined into the rear to extricate ourselves. It's been a long time since I rode in a vehicle, and I'm feeling a little winded as I plant myself on terra firma.

The girl, I notice, keeps her distance from the three of us. Her face wears a wary, alert expression.

We stand there, our little garden party gathered on the asphalt under a black sky freckled with stars.

"All right, Long Rider." This is in reference to my coat. I have to hand it to Uday. He's a master of nicknames. "Let's go inside."

I don't move. I let my arms dangle, the muscles loose, ready for action.

"I said let's go."

I watch him. "First, why don't you tell me what's going on?"

"Already told you, Gramps. It's movie night, and

you're the star. Hope you got a big dick, because our girl can handle it."

"That's not going to happen."

"You backing out?"

"I'm being realistic. Look around you. No motel."

"Yeah, well, we may have misled you about that."

"What else did you mislead me about?"

"Let's go in, and we'll talk about it."

"We can talk here. You didn't drive sixty miles out of the city just to watch me fuck your girl. What's really on the agenda?"

"Tell him, bro," Qusay says. "He's so fucking curious, let him know."

Uday shrugs. "Okay, Supertramp. It's like this. There are steam tunnels running underneath this whole complex, piping hot and cold air and water everyplace. A maze of them."

"Killmaze," Qusay adds. "That's what we call it."

"What *you* call it."

"Killmaze. We're the original steampunks."

"You don't even know what that means, dumb-ass."

"I know what it fuckin' means. I'm being creative with the language. I'm, like, reimagining words."

"Bullshit."

"That's your problem, bro. You got no poetry in your soul."

I clear my throat. "Fellows, could we stay on point?"

Uday refocuses on me. "Steam tunnels. A regular labyrinth. And you're our Theseus, if you know your mythology."

"Who's the minotaur?" I ask.

"Hey, you *do* know your mythology. What's down there is kind of a surprise. It won't be a happy surprise."

"So we're playing real-life Dungeons and Dragons."

For some reason this comment elicits stupid chuckles from the two of them. "You're not wrong, old man," Uday says.

"Suppose I don't want to play."

Uday pulls back his jacket to reveal the holstered weapon. "You don't have a choice."

I think he's wrong about that.

My next move is obvious. Grab Uday, who's closest to me. I can break his neck with one twist. Then use his gun to take out his brother. Even if Qusay is armed, he'll never be quick enough to draw and fire before I pop him.

I have no qualms about killing them. I've never had the least hesitation about killing anything, human or animal. Normal people have empathy, a conscience. For me, normality was never an option. I've known this all my life, known it ever since I saw my parents' shocked faces when they found the things I kept hidden at the bottom of my toy chest. I was seven years old.

Killing is pretty much the only thing I've ever been good at. And I guess I haven't lost my taste for it, either. I thought I had, but old habits die hard.

It should take all of five seconds to finish this pair, if I haven't lost a step. I'm about to do it when the girl says, "Stop."

It's the first time I've heard her voice, and I don't like it. It isn't the voice of the fairy-tale princess I signed on to protect.

I turn to her. She's drawn a pistol from her purse, and she's aiming it at me with a steady hand.

It looks as if her wide-open eyes weren't fearful, after all.

Shit. I've never been any damn good at reading women.

4

THERE'S NOTHING I CAN do now. I just stand there feeling stupid while Uday asks the girl what she's doing.

"He was getting set to bust a move on you," she says evenly.

"That so, Nowhere Man?"

I ignore the question. My attention is on her. "How'd you know?"

"You planted your feet a little wider apart. Setting your stance. It's a tell."

"I'll have to work on that."

"You won't get the chance," Uday says. "Pat him down, bro."

Qusay shrinks back. "Do I got to? He smells like day-old monkey meat."

"Just fucking *do* it."

Uday and the girl cover me. Qusay empties out the pockets of my duster, complaining the whole time. "Man, how long has it been since you bathed?"

It's been a while. My last shower was in a motel upstate, just before my money ran out. The seasons were different then.

The search yields nothing much. I've long since sold, pawned, or bartered anything of value.

Almost the only things I still own are my clothes—boots, jeans, a corduroy shirt stiff as cardboard, and the ankle-long duster, the kind of heavy all-weather coat that cowhands wear.

No, I never was a cowhand. But I do live outdoors, even if I'm not exactly riding the range.

"How long have you been tagging along on these outings?" I ask the girl.

"From the start. Every single time."

"How many times is that?"

"An even dozen. You make lucky number thirteen."

"How'd they ever find someone like you?"

"Wasn't hard. Lots of girls I know would be into it."

"Girls your age?"

"Or younger, even. We grow up fast, these days."

O brave new world, that has such fuckups in it.

Qusay strews the contents of my pockets on the asphalt. "It's just a bunch of shit. And no ID."

Uday looks me over. "What's your name, friend?"

"I'm nobody."

I don't like people knowing my name.

The girl steps forward. "He might be nobody now. But he used to be a big man in certain circles." She studies me. Her face is almost kind, but there is no light in her eyes. "Isn't that right, Mr. Shade?"

Slowly I nod.

"You know him?" Uday asks, astonished.

"Know *of* him. Like I say, he was kind of a player."

"This guy? You're shitting us."

"I'm not. He was a hitter. A pro. He racked up a lot of kills." Her eyes have never left me. "How many were there?"

"I didn't keep count." This is true.

"Back in the day he was one scary dude. I saw him once." She leans closer. "I saw you," she adds in a lower pitch.

"When?"

"I was twelve. So it would have been ten years ago. A party my folks gave. Backyard barbecue. You were there. My dad didn't think I knew about you. He didn't think I knew anything. But you know how kids are. They always have a way of finding out what their folks are up to."

"Yes," I say. "They always do."

"I heard him greet you that night. He called you Mr. Shade. But I had a feeling that wasn't your real name."

"It was an alias. One of several I used at the time."

"You came alone. I watched you the whole afternoon. You didn't say much. You seemed uncomfortable."

"I was."

"Why?"

"I've never exactly been part of society."

This is true. Even back then, when I was living in an apartment and not on the street, when I took daily showers and ate hot meals, I was still a wild creature at heart. I was like those half-domesticated wolves that can turn on their owners, or like some ex-cons I've known, men who spent most of their lives in prison and were never quite at ease in the wide-open world.

"Who is your father, anyway?" I ask her.

"Howard LeShawn."

That makes sense. LeShawn's a big-time lawyer who specializes in wealthy, disreputable clients. I think I remember that barbecue. I never was sure why I'd been invited. I worked for LeShawn at times, but I certainly didn't know him socially. Maybe he was afraid not to include me. Or maybe he wanted me there as a warning to others, a way of advising them not to mess with him. As the girl said, I had something of reputation ... back in the day.

"You mean," Uday says to the girl, "you knew all along we picked up a fucking hitman?"

"Not at first. He looks different now. But I thought I'd seen him somewhere." That explained the intensity of her gaze. "When he got out of the car, I recognized him. You should be glad I did."

Qusay shrugs. "He couldn't have done much. He's not carrying anything dangerous." He waves his hand over the scatter of items salvaged from my pockets. Ballpoint pen. Cigarette lighter. Folded up magazine. Balled up scarf.

The kid is wrong. Any one of those items can make a very serviceable weapon. But I didn't plan on using them. My hands would have been enough.

"I think he could do some damage even without a gun," the girl says. I'm beginning to think she's the only intelligent member of their group.

"Well, if that's so," Uday says, "we'd better

make sure he's under control."

He produces a pair of plastic handcuffs, the kind you can buy in bulk at seventy-five cents a pop. I guess I shouldn't be surprised that these two charmers would carry S & M gear.

Uday tosses the cuffs to his brother. "Hook him up."

"Shit, do I got to? I told you, I don't like touching him."

"Quit being all germophobic and get it done."

I hold out my arms. It's a lot easier to break free of plastic cuffs with your wrists in front of you. But Uday's wise to that trick.

"Behind his back," he says.

I let Qusay secure me. The plastic pinches tight.

"What I can't understand, Mr. Nobody," Uday says, "is why someone as streetwise as you would buy our bullshit."

"I didn't buy it."

"Then why go with us?"

I don't answer.

"Maybe he was hoping to jack our ride," Qusay says.

"No. That's not it." A thin smile rides the girl's lips. "He thought I was a damsel."

Short and to the point. Definitely the smartest of the bunch.

"That it, Liam Neeson?" Uday takes a step closer to me. "You have heroic designs making pretty pictures in your shaggy, lice-infested skull?"

He's wrong about the lice. I keep them away with menthol oil. Right about the rest of it, though.

Uday smiles. It's the first smile of genuine enjoyment I've seen on his face. "You dumb fuck. You really do think you're goddamned Sir Galahad."

Not anymore, I don't. If I'm a knight, I'm the Knight of the Woeful Countenance.

And I'm extremely disappointed in Dulcinea.

5

THE CONVERSATIONAL POSSIBILITIES HAVE been largely exhausted by this point. Qusay retrieves something from the BMW's trunk, and all three of them escort me up a short flight of stairs to the building's front door. Uday has a big set of keys, the kind a custodian would carry. This trio must have the run of the complex, not to mention a bought-and-paid-for security guard at the gate, or maybe more than one. They've turned this place into their own personal Disneyland.

With the door unlocked, I'm hustled inside. The room we enter is dark and small, unfurnished except for a card table and a couple of folding chairs. The lights stay off, either to avoid attracting attention or because power to this part of the fort is still off-line.

The item Qusay took from the car turns out to be a laptop computer. He sets it down on the table and flips up the lid. The screen comes on, washing the office in a pale sepia glow.

"Ordinarily," Uday says, reverting to tour-guide mode, "we don't provide our guests with a preview. Tonight I think we'll make an exception."

Qusay bends over the keyboard, working the trackpad. I look past them to the girl. "They'll get rid of you eventually, you know. They'll have to."

"Why is that?" she asks without interest.

"It's the one rule of men who kill—no witnesses."

"You would know about that," she says.

She's right. I do know about it. I know too much.

"Here we go." Qusay brings up a video, filling the screen.

Drawn by a certain morbid curiosity, I step forward for a better look. The video, though dim and grainy, stands out clearly against the darkness.

It's handheld camera footage, or so it seems. Shaky, stuttery. A point-of-view shot. Whoever is holding the camera moves in brief bursts of energy that punctuate stretches of stillness.

The location is the steam tunnels. I see pipes along the ceiling and walls. Long straightaways, dark side passages, sudden turns. No light anywhere. The camera operates in night-vision mode, rendering everything in shades of green.

It takes me a minute to realize that whoever's point of view I'm watching, it's not anything human.

A human being would stand taller, even in the cramped tunnels. And he would move differently. This is an animal, low to the floor, moving on all fours, its claws click-clacking on concrete. A dog or a big cat, maybe. On the prowl, following a scent.

"What the hell have you got down there?" I ask. "A leopard?"

"Sure," Uday says. "It's a remake of *Bringing Up Baby*."

First Beau Brummel, now Howard Hawks. The kid has to be an old movie buff. I'll bet he has TCM favorited on his DVR.

"How'd you convince it to wear a camera?" I ask.

"Tranquilizer dart. Then we strapped it to his head."

"Changing the batteries must be a pain."

"Power pack's tethered to the camera. Gives us five hours of live-streaming over Wi-Fi. After that, another dart."

The camera swerves left, plunging down a new corridor, another green-glowing schematic of geometrical tubing. It looks almost fake, a computer simulation.

There is movement ahead. A human figure. A man.

"Our most recent contestant," Uday says.

Great. He's a game show host now.

I see a blur of legs. The man is running all out, in pitch darkness. He can't have seen his pursuer, but he must have heard the telltale clacking of nails.

I know he can't go far without blundering into an obstacle. He should know it, too, but he's caught up in that final stage of panic that obliterates all rational thought. I can hear his rapid breathing as he sucks in shallow drafts of air, and the low, plaintive grunts that escape his throat.

Then he goes down. I can't tell what happened, whether he brained himself on an overhead pipe or tripped over his own feet. Either way, he's on the floor, scrabbling at concrete. His breathing comes harder, the gasps of a drowning man.

The camera moves in fast, like a zoom shot, a

twist of a telephoto lens. I catch a glimpse of the victim's face as he looks up. Young guy. Thin, almost gaunt. Bad teeth, rotten in his mouth. Probably a meth-head, someone the brothers picked up in a park or a public restroom, offering ready cash.

And he's screaming.

The sheer loudness of the screams takes me by surprise. I didn't realize the laptop's volume was turned up that high. His cries are big whooping howls that boomerang off the tunnel walls in clusters of echoes. I hear the drumroll of his shoes pounding the floor as he kicks, and the wild, hopeless slaps of his hands as he bats at the thing on top of him, a thing making other noises, worse noises—crunches and hungry gulps and thick slavering sounds.

The son of a bitch is being eaten alive. Being torn apart and swallowed, piece by piece, while he yells and kicks and flails.

"Look at him," Qusay says, leering in delight. "Doin' the paindance."

A gout of blood splashes the camera lens, erasing the imagery. Now the computer screen is only a dark rectangle, but the audio plays on. More screams, a choked gurgle, then no further sounds from the victim, only the slobber of feeding as the meal continues.

Qusay switches to the desktop view, brightening the screen's glow.

"How much of him was left?" I ask, holding my voice steady.

"Probably not a lot." Uday seems uncommonly cheerful about it. "There never is."

"You've done this to twelve men?"

"The dirty dozen. All losers like you. None of them will ever be missed."

"Aren't you worried somebody else will go down there and find that thing?"

"No one will find him. He hides out during the day. He knows we only feed him at night. And we always clean up his mess."

"Except for the last one," Qusay says.

Uday frowns, annoyed at the correction. "Yeah, we got a little careless there. But after tonight, we'll hose out Draco's lair."

That word again. "Why Draco?" I ask.

"Why not?"

"The constellation Draco represents a serpent. Whatever you've got down there is no snake. I heard its claws."

Uday lifts an eyebrow. "You know about the minotaur, and now Draco? I'm impressed. What sort of hitter were you?"

"The educated sort." This isn't true. I just have the kind of head that retains stray facts. "So it's some kind of reptile?"

"Could be."

"Alligator in the sewers? That kind of thing?"

"You're not far off, Tumbleweed Man. How about instead of playing Twenty Questions, you find out for yourself?"

A steel door stands at the rear of the office. Qusay depresses the push bar, and the door groans open.

"You're not going to uncuff me?" I ask.

Uday raises the other eyebrow. "Why, so you

can have a fighting chance?"

When he puts it that way, it does sound pretty ridiculous.

I approach the doorway. It frames a concrete landing, a tubular railing, a metal staircase descending into the gloom.

I'm standing on the threshold when something bites my leg. For an irrational moment I'm sure it's Draco—whatever the hell Draco might be. But it's only Qusay, kneeling behind me. He's knifed through my trouser leg, incising a long vertical gash in my right calf.

Blooded me. I've watched enough nature shows to understand why.

Uday knows what I'm thinking. "Draco hunts better when there's blood in the air."

"So do I."

"Big talk. But here's the bottom line, John Doe. You have no chance. Zero. You're going to die tonight."

"Looks that way."

I think it's the way I say it that makes him squint at me. "You don't even care, do you? You don't care about getting snuffed?"

"Vanity of vanities," I say. "All is vanity."

"What the fuck does that mean?"

The kid knows Beau Brummel and Howard Hawks, but not Ecclesiastes. Evidently there are gaps in his education.

"It means everything is bullshit. And if nothing's worth having, there's nothing to lose."

I begin to step through the doorway when the girl's voice stops me.

"You wouldn't have felt that way ten years ago."

I turn. In the glow of the computer screen she looks pale and willowy and very young.

"You're right. I wouldn't."

"What happened to you? How'd you end up like this?"

She seems honestly curious, unable to grasp how a man her father feared could become the stunted, shriveled figure before her.

"I'll tell you," I say, "if you tell me something first. What's your name?"

"My name? Why?" She flutters her eyelashes. "Are you in love?"

"Just tell me."

"I'm Scarlett. Fits me, right? The hair and all. But these guys call me Scar."

"That fits you better. Okay, Scar. It was six years ago. I was shaving. Watching my face in the mirror. It was afternoon, because I'd slept till noon—the way I usually did in those days."

"Move it along, old man," Qusay says, nudging me toward the landing.

"I finished the shave and patted the foam off my face, but I didn't stop looking in the mirror. It was like—like I'd never seen myself before. Like I was standing outside my own body, looking at a stranger. I saw that man, and he scared me. I had to get away from him. I put on this coat, walked out of my apartment, and never went back."

"You hit the road?" Scar asks. "Just like that?"

"Just like that."

"It doesn't make sense."

"Things rarely do."

"Who was your last target?"

"Some guy named Alex Dura."

"And it went down okay? It didn't go wrong?"

"I did the job and got paid."

The brothers have run out of patience. Unlike Scar, they have no interest in my personal history. Qusay gives me a harder shove, and this time I take the hint, crossing the threshold, leaving the office beyond.

Scar still stares after me, disappointed and perplexed. "So ... nobody's after you? You're not running from anyone?"

I look back, and I think I may be smiling. "I'm running from the man in the mirror. But I just can't seem to shake the son of a bitch."

The door shuts, and I'm in the dark.

6

I COULD HAVE FOUGHT back in the office, of course. Instead of meekly complying, I could have tried a few things. Sure, my hands are out of commission, but it's always possible to do some damage with a well-placed kick or a head-butt.

But I would have lost in the end, and they might have shot me right there.

I didn't want them to shoot me. I wanted to go into the tunnels. I want to face whatever monster they've got stashed away down here. And I want to kill it and kill it hard.

Until tonight, I thought I was all done with fighting. Lately I can't even remember what I used to be fighting for, back when my life still mattered. Another breath, another heartbeat? Another chance to take a piss or screw a woman? I wasn't kidding when I quoted Ecclesiastes. None of it means anything to me. None of it is worth a damn.

Even so, I want this fight. Because when Draco is dead, his masters will have to descend into the tunnels to take care of me.

And I will finish them. Uday and Qusay. Dead and deader.

And Scarlet, aka Scar. I read somewhere that redheads are slowly becoming extinct. I intend to hasten the process.

All three of them, who would take such pleasure in adding my last moments to their collection of torture-porn. I want to deny them that pleasure, and then deny them their lives.

It's the first thing I've wanted in a very long time. Before now, there's been nothing. No desire—neither the desire to go forward nor the desire to go back. Not even the desire to exist in the present moment. Only the dull routine of sleepwalking through my days, and the bad restless nights.

Now I have a purpose. My blood is up, and I've come back to life, like one of those horror movie monsters you can't keep down. I mean to win this battle.

And if it doesn't work out that way ... well, then I'll just get myself killed. Not the worst outcome.

It will be one way to stop the memories, and the bad dreams.

I stay on the landing for a moment or two. From behind the steel door I hear laughter. Two male voices and one female. All having great fun at my expense.

Laugh now, motherfuckers. I'll see to it you aren't laughing soon.

Slowly I go down the stairs, feeling my way, unable to grip the railing with my manacled hands.

God damn, it's hot in here. I mean, *really* hot. I guess there's a reason they're known as steam tunnels, right?

With each step I sink deeper into a bath of humid heat, thick and sloppy. By the time my boots touch bottom, I'm awash in a tickly trickle of perspiration. My corduroy shirt is already starting to soak through at the armpits and under the pecs. Sweat streaks my face like tears. I have to blink droplets out of my eyes.

The heat is bad, but right now the cuffs are my biggest problem. I've seen people pull their arms up under their feet to get their cuffed hands in front of them, but I lack the necessary flexibility. I've never exactly been a yoga enthusiast, and my fifty-two-year-old body is stiff and well used.

Still, I'll get the cuffs off somehow. I'm resourceful that way. Then I'll find or improvise a weapon. And beat the odds.

No doubt my twelve predecessors entertained similar notions. But they weren't me.

I start forward, down a long, narrow tunnel with a concrete floor, wet in patches. Debris crunches under my boots. I don't know what it is. It sounds like dry bones, but it's probably just old fast-food wrappers. Reality can be disappointingly prosaic.

I wish I had some way to see where I'm going. That cigarette lighter they confiscated would come in pretty handy right about now. If I'd been a Boy Scout, I could find two sticks and rub them together. Needless to say, I never was a Boy Scout.

Even in darkness, I can tell that the walls around me are crowded with pipes and cables feeding electricity and hot water to the two buildings open for business. Somewhere, a generator is working. I hear the faint ambient hum. No, not hear it—feel it. It vibrates through the floor.

Fuck, the tunnels are hot. Did I mention that? The atmosphere is sweltering, tropical, thick with the humidity of a greenhouse or a rain forest.

I've never been a fan of hot climates. Miami, Phoenix, Palm Springs—they never were my haunts, even when I had the money and leisure to travel. Maybe it's my ancestry, all those clannish, clammy Scots on my father's side, and those rehabilitated Vikings at the root of my mom's family tree. Or maybe it was hearing too many Sunday school sermons about hell and damnation, the eternal thirst and the worm that will not die. Even as a kid, I suspected that if there was a hell, I would be going there.

It looks like I've arrived.

My oilskin coat is all wrong for this environment. Sweat is bubbling on my skin, soaking into my shirt and pants. If I can't get the coat off, I may die of dehydration before Draco even gets near me. And I can't lose the coat unless I can defeat the cuffs.

I go on. My mind keeps returning to what I said to Scar. It's the first time I've told that story out loud. But I didn't tell all of it. I left out the most important part.

I left out Rebecca.

There are few virtues I can call my own, but one of them is honesty with myself. And with you, my imaginary friend. I can be straightforward with you. And so I can share with you a truth that's obvious even to a person of my limited capacity for introspection.

Rebecca stood behind the man I saw in the mirror.

No, I didn't see her then. But I've seen her

many times since, in those bad dreams of mine. She comes at night. She haunts me. Maybe there's no escape from her, except in death. And even then ... what dreams may come ... you know the score.

Sometimes I hate that bitch. I really do.

Even if she was my daughter.

The darkness solidifies with a thud, and I find myself walking, Mr. Magoo-like, into a wall. I've come to a fork in the tunnel. Arbitrarily I go to the right. This turns out to be a bad decision. A few yards in, my foot comes down on something slick. Without my hands to protect me, I can only crash forward on both knees. The hard concrete doesn't do my aging kneecaps any favors, but the blow is softened by what feels like a mess of Jell-O and a scatter of rags.

Exploring the pile as best I can with my cuffed hands, I feel torn strips of cotton and denim, a pair of half-disintegrated shoes, and, strewn throughout, small lightweight cubes like dice.

The cubes are teeth. I figure this out when I'm holding a bicuspid in my hand.

These are the earthly remains of the poor son of a bitch I watched on video. Qusay did say they'd forgotten to clean up.

What I've stumbled upon is a gastric pellet. Some predators regurgitate the parts of their prey that they can't digest. In this case, clothes and footwear and teeth. The slick coating with the texture of gelatin is a glaze of mucus coughed up with the rest of the stuff.

You may wonder how I know all this. No, I've

never been a hunter—well, not a hunter of animals, anyway.

But when I was living a more conventional life, I watched my share of TV. I liked to lie back in my recliner with a freshly shaken Manhattan and flip through the two billion channels on my satellite dish. A lot of times, I stopped on a nature documentary, because nature shows hit my sweet spot —painlessly informative, adequately diverting. Remember how I said I have the kind of mind that absorbs stray facts?

So I know stuff. I know that the Great Barrier Reef is the largest living structure on earth. An individual blood cell requires sixty seconds to take a lap around the human body. It's the male seahorse who gets pregnant. The human eye blinks 4.2 million times per year. The earth weighs in at a svelte 6.6 sextillion tons. A mosquito has forty-seven teeth. A cockroach can live for several weeks without a head.

Like a politician, ha ha.

Anyway, the gastric pellet gives me some useful info. It tells me that whatever I'm up against is related to birds and reptiles. They're the ones who cough up gastric pellets.

And the thing is big. Damn big. It swallowed the guy from head to toe, at least one hundred twenty pounds of food.

What size must it be, if it can hold that much in its belly? The size of a goddamn shark.

The old *Saturday Night Live* routine comes back to me—doorbell rings; mystery voice chirps, "Candygram." Punchline: unsuspecting homeowner is eaten by a foam rubber land shark.

Big laughs.

Unsteadily I get to my feet and move on. In the short time I've been underground, I've already picked up a couple of pointers. One is to stay in a half crouch at all times. The ceiling height varies unpredictably, and keeping low is the only way to avoid a head-on collision with one of the low-hanging conduits that drip from the ceiling like stalactites. That's a lesson I learned the painful way.

Here's another useful tip, in the unlikely event that you should ever find yourself in my situation. In this smothering heat, you have to pace yourself. At first, I moved too fast, got a little winded, and a surreal swooning sensation came over me. Though I succeeded in staying upright, I learned not to press my luck. The tunnels, with their heat and darkness and claustrophobic boundaries, aren't meant for speed. Down here, even slow progress comes hard.

So what? Everything comes hard. That's life. People say the world is divided into good and evil. Not me. My world is divided into strength and weakness. Weakness is the only unpardonable sin. It can masquerade as virtue—the meek will inherit the earth, and all that happy crap—but in reality it's only an open door to the wolves among us, the ones who take ruthless advantage of any frailty.

You know, wolves like me.

Throughout my life I've simply grabbed whatever I wanted and disposed of anything that got in my way. Law of the jungle—the strongest beast rules. It's part of my DNA, I think. Can't blame my folks. They were fine, caring people saddled with an impossible child. I never loved them, but that's only because I've never loved anyone. No need to feel sorry for me about that, if you're inclined to. I'm like a man born blind; it might seem sad that I've never seen the sunset, but I'm okay with it, since I have no idea what I'm missing.

They didn't abuse me, and I wasn't raised in poverty or anything close to it. My dad was a dentist, for Christ's sake, with Norman Rockwell prints on his waiting-room walls. My sister and brother turned out fine. Get the picture? I'm the bad seed.

So what does a young man do when he grows up without some vital human component that lets him relate to others? If he has a taste for cruelty and a certain natural talent for violence, he starts to mix with a certain sort of people, and those people eventually decide they have a use for that young man. Killers aren't rare. But killers who can keep a cool head are hard to find.

I've never pretended to be better than I am. Julie, now—Julie's different. She makes excuses. She likes to believe she's better than she is. She thinks if she doesn't admit the truth to herself, it won't be true.

Julie's my ex. Not an ex-wife, merely an ex-significant other. There've been no wives. I never had the inclination to marry her or anyone else. I'm not just a wolf; I'm a lone wolf.

Other women played a part in my life. But Julie will always be special. She's the only one who gave me a child.

And yet ... not really. I mean, yes, Rebecca was mine. But Julie never let me play a part in the girl's life. She closed the door on me. Said she couldn't let Rebecca be tainted by someone like me. Tainted. That was the word she used. How often do you hear that one in conversation?

But as I said, her own hands were far from clean. Nobody who ran in our circles was clean. She persuaded herself that her sins were venial, while mine were mortal. But we both worked for the same people. We both cashed checks underwritten by the same fictitious corporations.

She's a CPA, a talented one, who helped launder the money and fix the books. She could have made a living in an honest line. But not quite such a good living as she made with Howard LeShawn.

She thought herself superior to me because there was no blood on her hands. I told her, Don't kid yourself. Where do you think the numbers on those spreadsheets come from? You know how many people have to die in order to keep this operation profitable?

But she wouldn't see it. Some people are like that. They compartmentalize.

Me, I had no pretenses. I've always known just who and what I am. A psychopath is characterized by narcissism, antisocial behavior, anger management issues, lack of empathy and conscience, and a tendency to manipulate others. Check, check, double check.

Anyway, as soon as she saw the telltale second line on her pregnancy test, Julie parted company with me. Afterward, she kept our baby to herself, never let me near. As if I had a contagious disease. Or as if I were the contagion itself.

I let her do it. I gave in to another person, just that once. And so I couldn't know my own child. That in itself isn't the greatest tragedy of my life.

But it didn't end there.

I've traveled maybe another two hundred yards, turning again when the tunnel hooks left, when I hear a noise, not far away, and drawing nearer.

The tapping of nails on concrete.

That was quick.

Whatever lives down here must have quite an appetite.

7

The noise comes from up ahead, a faint clickety-clack, reminding me of a train set I had when I was a kid. I haven't thought of that train set in years. Truth be told, I never played with it very much. Even at that age, I had a taste for darker pastimes. The fire in the Deweys' house down the street, the one that took out their front porch ... Yeah, that was me. And the Watsons' dog, the one that always snapped and growled at me, the one that was found with a sharpened stick rammed in its throat? Me again.

Am I supposed to be relatable? An antihero with a cynical exterior and a heart of gold? Get real. Any man who kills for money was born bent out of shape.

Oddly enough, the memory of the Watsons' dog helps stiffen my spine. I've killed an animal before. True, it was only a small dog. But I was only a small boy. Now I'm all grown up.

I crouch there, dripping sweat, peering into darkness, my hands trapped behind me, as I listen to the approach of something unknown and predatory, something almost supernatural in its faceless, nameless strangeness.

Draco.

Clicking nails.

I feel the way our ancestors must have felt when they gathered around a communal fire and heard the noises of the jungle, imagining the unseen dangers just beyond the reach of the fire glow. But they had tools, weapons, freedom of action. They weren't being delivered to a predator trussed and helpless, a sacrificial victim, a staked goat.

I have to get my hands free. It's my only chance. Maybe there's something on the floor that can help. There's all kinds of debris in these tunnels. I need something that can saw or slice. A sharpened screw, a metal shard. Anything that cuts plastic.

I drop to my knees, groping as best I can.

The clicking and clacking sounds are louder now. Rapid and regular like the tick of a mechanical heart. An urgent, hungry sound.

And along with it, a kind of snuffling, a low, heavy breathing as the thing follows my scent. I can picture its snout low to the floor, a ribbon of drool unspooling from its mouth.

Still kneeling, I scramble closer to the wall. One of the pipes brushes my sleeve. Hot. The pipe is packed with steam, and over the years the insulation has worn off.

And there it is. My chance.

I shove myself into position, my back to the wall, and press the plastic handcuffs against the pipe. Heat radiates from it like the flare of a blowtorch. My wrists are getting singed, and all I can do about it is grit my teeth.

The creature shambles closer. I see a faint red luminescence winking on and off against the blackness. At first I think it's some trick of the vision, like the webworks of color you see when you rub your eyelids.

No, it's real. And I know what it is. The creature is rigged with a camera, right? The blinking red light is an LED, signaling that the camera is active.

My three amigos are watching me right now, in real time, in the office. They can see me better than I can see myself. The camera, in infrared mode, registers me as a green blur of body heat.

"Fuckers," I say, just loud enough that they may be able to hear. The camera does have a microphone, after all.

I hold the cuffs rigidly in place while the plastic strap deforms under the heat, buckling, stretching.

The animal is very close to me now. I can smell its garbage-pail breath, the reek of old bones and rotten meat.

It stops about three yards away. In the dim red flickering light I have an indistinct impression of small glittery eyes and a broad, flat skull. It's watching me, sizing me up. For a moment it holds off its attack.

The other victims must have run when they saw it. I'm staying put. My behavior is unexpected, confusing.

The LED swings restlessly from side to side. The creature is turning its head back and forth, with the laziness of a cat's swishing tail.

I feel the plastic tear in one spot. Almost free.

From deep in the animal's throat comes a hissing noise. It must be tensing to pounce.

I pull harder at the cuffs, straining the half-melted plastic.

And it strikes.

In a rush of speed it comes at me, all clacking claws and hot breath and feral stink.

I kick out against the wall and spin clear. I hit the floor on my back and feel something snap. Not bone, thank you very much. Plastic. The cuffs have come apart. My hands are free.

Now all I need is a weapon—and a plan.

Flashback: a night, decades ago, when I was a younger man. An unarmed man, in the wrong place, an alley that dead-ended at a brick wall. Behind me, a crunch of footsteps, the snick of a pistol's slide. I was being hunted, and though I'd found a hiding place, the hunter was close.

He was a yard away when I tossed a trash can lid out of the shadows. He pivoted toward the spiral of movement, and I was all over him, wielding a chunk of wood torn from a pallet crate. Long nails, still embedded in the wood, sank deep into his skull.

Distract and attack. A viable strategy, then and now.

I unbuckle my belt and jerk it out of the loops.

There's a risk in doing this. I've lost weight on my sabbatical. Without the belt, my pants may drop down to my ankles. Not only will this impede my movement, but it will give my unseen spectators a good laugh. My final moments may make it into some perverse blooper reel.

But my pants stay on, preserving my dignity, such as it is. I wrap one end of the belt around my fist. A wide belt, thick leather, with a large steel buckle that swings like a pendulum.

I still can't see the animal. I know it has legs and a low belly. When I jumped clear, it brushed against me, and I felt the dry leathery texture of its skin—hairless, creased and crinkled, rough like sandpaper.

It's moving toward me now. The LED gives me a target. Uday said the camera was strapped to the creature's head. Aim for the camera, and I may just smack the creature in the face. At the very least I may smash the lens and put a damper on all the fun.

I wait for it to make its move. In the LED's winking light, I catch hints of its anatomy. Splayed legs. Wagging dewlap. Ropey, muscular neck. Body long and low like an alligator ...

An alligator in the sewers.

Uday's voice comes back to me: You're not far off, Tumbleweed Man.

I have it now.

I know.

No time to think about it. The creature barrels at me, closing fast.

I snap the belt like a whip. The buckle connects. I feel the impact, hear the damp thud of contact.

The animal jerks away, dragging its thick body backward. I lash the belt again, aiming at the LED that floats in space.

My second attempt misses the mark. I reel in

the belt as the creature, emboldened, comes at me in another rush.

Holding the belt in both hands, I snap the leather strip hard in its face.

Again it withdraws. I haven't really hurt it, but I've taken it by surprise.

Distract—and attack.

I charge. Before the animal can react, I lunge for its throat, wielding the steel buckle like a dagger. The hook on that buckle is sharp enough to do real damage if delivered with sufficient force.

As the creature swings toward me, I pound the buckle into its neck.

The hook catches. I pull the buckle downward, grooving a ragged cleft in the thing's scaly flesh.

The creature makes an ugly, angry spitting noise, a hissing cockroach. I wrest the buckle free and hop back, barely avoiding the snakelike whip of its neck as its jaws snap.

Something strikes at my legs. The tail, lashing.

The blow from the tail almost knocks me down. If I lose my footing, the animal will be on top of me. Game over.

I don't fall. Before it can strike again, I sling one leg over the low hill of its back, straddling it, and I bring the steel buckle down, hammering the hook into its shoulder, ripping out long strips of hide.

The animal bucks and seizes, struggling to throw me off. I hold on, my knees clamped on its ribs, and dig in with the steel prong again and again as the thing spits in delirious rage.

With a final roiling spasm, it shakes me loose. I

stick the landing, staying on my feet, and retreat, putting distance between myself and the enemy in case it resumes the attack.

It doesn't. It's had enough. The LED swims away from me, the claws clicking furiously as the creature withdraws along the passageway in the direction it had come.

I've beaten it. For now, anyway. I've hurt it, made it bleed. There's blood on my hands, the monster's blood.

I forgot just how good it can feel—the raw and primal thrill of single combat. Bearding the sabertooth in its den, felling the gladiator in the arena, besting the enemy who would have claimed your life.

"How do you like that, you motherfuckers?" I shout, addressing not the creature but its masters above ground.

8

MY NEWLY LIBERATED WRISTS sting like a bastard. I was bitten by fire ants once, while on a junket to Houston. Fucking Texas. You know they have flying cockroaches there? Jesus.

Anyway, that pain was a lot like this. I massage some circulation into the wrists and manage to twist the remnants of the cuffs off my arms.

After snugging the belt around my waist, I finally shed the coat. It's the first time I've had it off in months. Irrationally I hate to lose it. It's been part of me for so long, it feels like a second skin. But even a snake has to molt some time. I unbutton the flaps, drop the coat, and try to convince myself I feel cooler, but in this subterranean inferno, even losing a thick layer of clothing makes less difference than you'd think.

I fold up the coat, doing a neat job of it because my mother taught me that neatness counts, and leave it by the wall. If I survive my ordeal, I'll retrieve it later.

Then I examine the damage to my leg, the one Qusay slashed. The cut isn't deep, but it's been bleeding freely, oozing down to my ankle and soaking through my sock. I tear off a shirtsleeve and tie it around my leg, below the knee, making a tourniquet. Probably it will stanch the flow. Not that it matters much. The animal knows my scent.

Yes. The animal.

Draco.

I know what it is now. I know what I'm up against.

Sir Galahad, indeed.

As I mentioned, I've seen a lot of nature shows. The ones I'm thinking of at the moment involve a handful of islands in the Indonesian archipelago, where an endangered species still haunts the rainforest, bringing down water buffalo, goats, and the occasional unlucky squid fisherman trudging back to his village with his catch. The biggest reptile still alive on earth, the closest thing to a dinosaur in the modern world.

The Komodo dragon lizard.

Larger than an alligator, growing as long as ten feet from the end of the tail to the tip of the snout. Heavily muscled and solidly built, weighing up to two hundred fifty pounds, and able to consume two-thirds of its own weight in one meal. Sluggish and torpid most of the time, but capable of frantic bursts of speed. I once saw a clip from some crazy Japanese game show where an intrepid female contestant had to outrace a Komodo dragon across an open field. She made it, but just barely. And in the dark tunnels, with walls springing up everywhere, I can't make that kind of speed.

Darkness isn't a hindrance to a dragon lizard. It relies primarily not on its eyesight, which is restricted to detecting movement, or its hearing, which is so poor that the animal was once thought to be deaf, but on its deeply forked tongue, which continually flicks out of its mouth, literally tasting the air. The creature has something called Jacobson's organ in the roof of its mouth, which can read molecules collected by the probing tongue and pick up the scent of blood from six miles away.

I've seen footage of Komodos drawn like sharks to a bloodied victim, arriving one after another until the doomed animal is hemmed in by a circle of flat, staring, matte-black eyes and cruel jaws festooned with ropes of pink saliva. The fangs in those jaws face backward, permitting a stronger grip—the Komodo can bite down hard enough to snap a man's leg—and the glands in the mouth secrete an anticoagulant. Once bitten, the victim is left with a wound that won't heal, leaking blood that can't clot. Slowly but inexorably he'll bleed out. As his blood pressure drops and he starts to lose consciousness, the Komodo moves in to strip the skin and wolf down the entrails, even as the victim struggles feebly, half-awake, in a stupor of blood loss and numbing pain.

So that's my adversary. Draco—a name that can signify a serpent, but also a dragon. I really should have figured that out sooner.

As I recall, knights who killed dragons sometimes ended up with sainthood. So I got that going for me, as Bill Murray might say.

It would be interesting to know just how Uday and Qusay got hold of this particular pet. Komodos aren't the kind of item you pick up at your local PetSmart. But anything can be purchased for a price. I know all about that. In a world where human life is a marketable commodity, I can't be surprised that an exotic species of monitor lizard is for sale by somebody somewhere.

I think this through, dispassionately enough, and then abruptly I'm shaking all over in a series of tremors that rattle me like seismic shocks. At first I don't even know what it is. Some sort of emotional meltdown, delayed reaction, panic attack? Then I feel my hands curl into fists, and I know.

It's rage.

I don't hate the animal. It's only an instrument. I hate Uday and Qusay and Scar, the unholy trinity who arranged this horror show to serve as televised sport. I've killed people, and I made it painful when it was necessary to make them talk, but I'd never turned it into a game. I may be destined for someplace pretty close to the lowest rung of hell, but there'll be a few circles beneath me, and the people who made the steam tunnels into their own personal Jurassic Park will belong there. They're worse human beings even than I am, which is saying something.

I start forward again. Proceeding in the direction the animal has gone may not seem like the best idea, but look at it this way. If I go back, I'll end up where I started. I already know there are no exits that way. On the other hand, there may be an exit somewhere ahead. Maybe none of my predecessors ever made it that far.

Besides, I can't just wait around until Draco sniffs me out again. He will, you know. Komodos are an endangered species, but this particular specimen isn't nearly endangered enough. I inflicted harm, but I didn't kill him. And from everything I know about Komodo dragons, courtesy of the Discovery Channel and Animal Planet, I expect him to try again very soon. Komodos are tenacious as hell. They may back off for a while, but they don't quit. They have the inhuman patience of all predators, and when their small, evil brains lock on to a target, they stick to it, no matter what. The smackdown I delivered won't deter the dragon for long.

Not to mention, I'm the only large prey down here. The only item on the menu. Komodos can go for a long time without eating, but not forever. A few stray rats aren't going to satisfy a predator of his size.

Draco has to come after me if he wants to stay alive.

9

SO I MOVE ON, groping my way as before. Ordinarily, when you're in the dark for a while, your eyes adjust and you start to make out dim shapes. But that's because there's always some ambient light. Down here, there's no light at all, and no way for my eyes to adjust. My pupils are already as dilated as they're going to get, and I can't see jack shit.

That, incidentally, was one of my aliases: Jack Shit. I kid you not. When I was starting out in the business, someone tagged me with that one.

You're a cold one, kid, the guy told me, with a grudging note of admiration. *You don't give jack shit about nothing.*

The name stuck. Or I should say, it stuck until I started making a go of it as a hitter. After that, people became more circumspect, and the dumb gibes stopped. Too bad, really. I kind of liked that name.

And no, my first name isn't Jack. As I said, I don't like people knowing my identity. Think of me as a low-rent version of Clint Eastwood in a Sergio Leone western, the Bum with No Name.

Not that it matters what you know about me. You don't even exist. You're a figment of my imagination. I've spent the past six years talking to you in my head.

Why not? It's not as if I can talk to anyone else. All the people I knew in my past life, the people I worked for, must assume I'm dead. Which is just as well. If they knew I was alive, they might want to track me down and shut me up. A man like me knows many secrets. That's okay as long as he's reliable. But when he gets all flaky—when he does something crazy like trading in a cushy, affluent life for the hobo trade—then he becomes a distinct liability. Best to take no chances with him.

They say Wall Street types value predictability above all. They want to know what IBM and Ginnie Mae will be doing tomorrow and next year. They don't like surprises. My bosses were the same way. They hired me not because I was the world's stealthiest assassin or greatest marksman, but because they could count on me to behave in a conventionally self-interested manner. I was a rational actor. There were plenty of people who were handier with a gun or smarter or smoother, but those people couldn't be trusted. They were always getting coked up or blabbing to some hooker or welshing on a deal. I was sufficiently boring and unimaginative to be trustworthy. My mediocrity was my shield. You don't hire an assassin who's cleverer and cagier than you; there's no telling what he might do.

Howard LeShawn was only one of several people who employed my services as needed. I worked freelance, an independent contractor. Small business is the backbone of America, you know.

My employers were moderately big-time operators who moved cocaine, meth, heroin, and pot onto the streets and playgrounds of America, while diversifying into other leisure services like prostitution and gambling. Some of what they did was legal, but all of it was built on a foundation of drug money and sex traffic and heavyset guys who'd bombed out in the fight game and now made their money working over unlucky gamblers who owed the wrong people. LeShawn and the others were rough men, men who could order a hit as casually as the average Joe orders a take-out dinner. They could have a man and his wife killed, and sleep soundly that night. I'm not judging them. I was the same. Worse, maybe, since I did the killing myself.

How did I get on this subject? Oh, yeah. Jack Shit. Funny how the mind works. How it wanders ...

Anyway, when we last left our hero, he was trudging blindly through a maze of steam tunnels in the suffocating heat. We pick up our tale a few minutes later—or an hour, I really can't say—when he discovers a new surprise in his path.

I kick it by accident, a low mound, soft and crumbly. I have a good idea what it is even before I kneel to make an examination. It has the texture of dry earth, mixed with small, sharp chips that are fragments of bone.

Speaking of shit ...

Yeah, that's right. This is another part of Draco's last meal, the part he was able to digest. He crapped it out onto the floor, and it dried into a large clayey mass. From those nature shows and my retentive memory, I know Komodos freely mix stool and urine in their droppings. Though I can't see it, I know the stool will be dark, and the dried uric acid will be white. All of it is powdery and only mildly foul-smelling.

You may not believe it, but stumbling across that pile of poop is the best thing that's happened to me all night. This is my chance to go all Bear Grylls and put some of my reality TV learning to use.

I take off my boots, then my socks, and put one sock inside the other—a necessary precaution inasmuch as each sock is too liberally dotted with holes to serve as a carrying case without reinforcement. Then I break off handfuls of excrement and stuff them into the pouch I've made. When I'm done, I have a sock crammed with lizard shit, the kind of gift Santa might leave for the world's naughtiest child.

My boots go back on. I explore the walls, feeling everywhere, until I find a rectangular box protruding from a vertical pipe. I have no clue as to its purpose—thermostat, pressure gauge, junction box—but I'm hoping there are live wires inside. I pry off the front panel, which isn't hard to do, because it's only thin plastic, and find a nest of wires which I pull apart. I touch the tips together at random until I make a spark.

Hallelujah.

Ever hear of buffalo chips? They're clumps of dried dung, high in methane. They can be used to start campfires.

A Komodo dragon is not a buffalo, but I'm guessing its digestive system is just as gassy. What I've made is a tinder bundle. It ought to catch fire easily enough.

I test my theory by shoving the open end of the sock into the box while I spark the wires again.

It takes a few tries, but I'm rewarded by a faint bluish glow in my little bag of shit. The top layer of excrement has ignited. As I watch, it heats up to a dull red. It doesn't produce a lot of light, but at least I won't be blundering into any more walls for a while.

"Grok make fire," I say out loud in a caveman voice. Immediately I regret it. It's not that I have anything against talking to myself. I do it all the time. I'm doing it right now.

It's just that the line sounded a whole lot funnier in my head.

10

I CAN MOVE FASTER now, guided by the light. I feel the need to give my invention a name. I like naming things, remember?

The pioneers had all sorts of terms for buffalo flop in its capacity as fuel. Plains oak. Prairie coal. The French called it *bois de vache*, wood of the buffalo, which would make what I've got *bois de dragon*. But screw the French. I prefer the Sioux term: nik-nik.

My nik-nik bag keeps burning fiercely, with a pungent, peppery smell. Periodically I have to stir the embers and scrap off a layer of ash, using the lid pried from the mystery box.

About fifty yards on, I reach another intersecting passage marked by a riot of spray-painted graffiti left by some intrepid tunnel rat—not one of my fellow victims, just some urban adventurer who'd sneaked in here after the base closed down.

ABBANDEN HOPE, it reads, a garish misspelling two feet high.

Somehow the sentiment seems appropriate to my circumstances.

For no special reason I go to the right, leaving the other passageway unexplored. To be honest, I'm not putting much thought into my navigational decisions. I'm thinking again of the story I told Scar, the story that became strangely objective when spoken aloud.

What I saw in the mirror really did scare me. But maybe it shouldn't have. Maybe what I saw was only the simple truth, cold reality. I always prided myself on being a realist. People would say to me, *You do the shit no one else will touch.* And I would say with a shrug, *Somebody's got to.*

As an answer, it wasn't much. As a philosophy of life, it was even less. It was a rote response, a conversational tic. An evasion, really. A tough-guy quip substituting for thought and insight.

Now I wonder—as I meander through the stifling dark, guided by my luminous bag of dung—I wonder how much of my former life consisted of similar avoidance techniques. How much of it was rationalization, self-deception, or simply refusing to think very much about who I was and what I did? How much thinking did I do, really? Or was it all just going through the motions, reading scripted lines, playing a part?

Sleepwalking. Sleepwalking through the decades, killing and killing again, and never coming to terms with it, never letting it be real.

For the man in the mirror it was real. He, at least, wasn't a somnambulist. I stared into his wide-open eyes—my eyes—open at last, and for the first time.

Of course he scared me. The truth may set you free, but most of the time it scares the piss out of you first.

I don't know. I could have it all wrong. I don't

even know why I'm telling you this. Oh, yes. Because of what I said to Scar. Scar, who saw me at LeShawn's barbecue ten years ago.

I barely remember the event. It was one of many social functions I reluctantly attended in those days. Was Julie there? I can't say. She probably was. LeShawn would have invited her. And he wouldn't have been conscious of any awkwardness in bringing us together. He knew nothing about our past. No one did.

She'd kept it a secret, and I'd respected her wishes. This may actually be the only decent thing I ever did. Well, until I decided to save Scar tonight. And we've seen how that worked out.

My chivalrous impulse toward Julie didn't pay off any better. I let her decide things. When I ran into her at parties—at barbecues—I didn't challenge her decisions. I didn't make a scene. I didn't take her aside and start an argument or even plead my case. I let her have her way. Admittedly, I spied on Rebecca a few times when she was a child. But Julie found out and went ballistic. After that, I never intruded again.

I guess I thought I was doing the right thing. If so, I miscalculated. A lot of grief could have been avoided if I'd been a little less understanding and a little more of an asshole.

Ironic, isn't it? I was an asshole in every other aspect of my life, but in the one department where it mattered, I chose to be the good guy. And look where it got me, Julie.

Look where it got us both.

Waving my nik-nik bag around, letting its ruddy

glow travel over the walls and floor, I catch sight of a distant crosshatched shape. I approach it, and it resolves into a ladder bolted to the wall.

The ladder rises into a narrow shaft cut into the ceiling. I hang onto the lower rungs, peering upward into the shaft, and in the glow of my makeshift lantern I dimly perceive a circle of metal at the top, about twelve feet off the floor.

A manhole cover.

All right, now we're getting somewhere.

I climb the ladder, place the bag on the highest rung, and explore the cast iron lid directly overhead. It's heavy as hell, but I don't think it's fixed in place. With enough muscle, I can shove it off. Then haul myself out of this hellhole and leave Draco behind.

And after that? I could just go on my way, of course. It would be hours before the three snuff-video fans realize Elvis has left the building. But I don't plan on doing that. I plan to double back to the office and take them by surprise. They won't have their guns out. They'll think they're safe.

That's when the target is always most vulnerable—when he thinks he's safe.

All that is in the future. First I've got to get the manhole cover off. The thing must be a hundred pounds or more, and who knows what sort of debris may have collected on top of it, further weighing it down?

Still, where there's a will, there's a way. That's another thing my mother taught me. A very practical woman, my mother. As you might expect, she was awfully disappointed in me.

I press my palms against the lid and strain with my shoulders, my back. Nothing.

Got to put more effort into it. I've never been into weightlifting or workouts, but I'm one of those freakish types with naturally exaggerated upper-body strength. Even as a kid, I could do pull-ups effortlessly. I'm guessing that even in my current debilitated state, I can still bench two hundred pounds, more than enough to get the job done. Theoretically, that is. The practical problem is leverage. Balanced on the ladder, pushing straight up, I'm in the wrong position to exert maximum force.

I shove harder and feel a momentary shift in time with a rasp of metal on stone. The lid has moved. Not much, maybe an inch, but I've exposed a paper-thin arc of sky. Starlight leaks through, augmenting the glow of the bag.

This is going to work. Until this moment I don't think I really believed I would get out of the tunnels. I've been playing a game of pretend with myself, acting as if I had a chance. The only way to keep up morale, you know. Sometimes you need to tell yourself a little lie just to keep going.

I'm not lying now. I really think I'm about to make good on my escape. One or two more good shoves, and I can ease the lid out of position and squirm through. Years on the road have left me a skinny bastard. I don't need a lot of room to maneuver.

I place my hands on the lid, tensing for another try, and then Draco's got me by the leg.

11

Son of a bitch ...

To be honest, in my concentration on the manhole, I've pretty much forgotten about my friendly neighborhood dinosaur. But he hasn't forgotten me. While I've been standing on the ladder, my boots six feet off the floor, Draco has slipped into the shaft and started to climb.

Evidently he can be stealthy when he wants to be. Anyway, I didn't hear any clicking of toenails. And with my focus directed upward, I didn't see the red LED or smell his open-sewer breath.

He's scaled the ladder one rung at a time, pulling himself erect with his powerful foreclaws. He must be about six feet long from nose to hindquarters, with another three or four feet of tail. Now he's stretched out vertically on the ladder, his hind feet on the floor, his front feet two rungs below mine, and he's got my leg in his jaws.

My right calf, the one Qusay bloodied. Maybe the smell of the wound made him home in on that spot.

I told you that Komodos can exert serious bite pressure. I did not lie. The sudden eruption of pain hits me like an electric shock.

My knees buckle, and I lose my footing, and

now I'm being dragged down the ladder, bumping my chin on the rungs, getting banged up and bruised as the dragon waddles backward, pulling me with him as he reverses out of the shaft. The nik-nik bag falls with me, painting red spirals in the dark.

I hit the floor and grab wildly for anything to hold on to, but there's nothing, and now I'm sliding out of the shaft and into the main part of the tunnel, helpless on my belly. As soon as the animal has me in the clear, he's going to be right on top of me, splitting my guts with his teeth and slobbering over my entrails while I thrash and kick.

Doin' the paindance, Qusay called it.

Prick.

The thought of Qusay and the realization that he and the other two can see me right now—that they're watching on video and laughing as I'm jerked along the floor like a chew toy—this thought slaps me out of my stupor and gets my mind humming again.

Land shark, I think. I wasn't so far off with that image. How do you repel a shark? Unless the good people behind Shark Week were lying to me all those years, you punch the hungry motherfucker in the nose.

I cock one leg and deliver a kick with a steel-toed boot, aiming square at the dragon's snout.

Doesn't work. Draco holds on to the other leg as he shakes his head irritably from side to side, tossing me around like a rat in a terrier's mouth.

We're almost entirely clear of the shaft now. Another second, and the goddamn bastard will have me where he wants me.

I draw back my leg and kick again.

This time I really feel the impact. The first kick only grazed him. The second one slams hard into bone.

And he lets go.

The big jaws spring open. I roll clear before they can clamp down again. I have no idea what kind of damage he's done to my leg, but it's bad enough that I nearly slip on a stripe of my own blood as I try to stand. Even so, I get to my feet, ignoring the sizzle of pain that begins at my ankle and ends at my hip.

I can't run. Can't hide. Can barely fight. My belt won't stop him again.

Basically, by any rational standard, I'm fucked.

But I'm not the rational type. And I still think Draco is mine.

After all, I know his name.

12

THE NIK-NIK BAG HAS landed close by, and in its glow I can see my adversary clearly for the first time.

He's looking at me, and I'm looking back. It occurs to me that the dragon, in predator mode, will be triggered to action by any sudden movement on my part. As long as I remain still, he may delay his attack.

I ought to do something. But I can't think of any moves left to make. And the sight of the creature holds me strangely spellbound. I think it's the face that fascinates me—the flat, grinning, primeval face, with the long yellow tongue flicking again and again, the forked tip tasting the air. That face with its dead black shark's eyes and its long jaws studded with shark's teeth and strands of saliva, dangling like tinsel. The face wrinkling into the neck's deep folds of scaly hide, losing blood where I gouged it—but not too deeply, because those scales are backed by a meshwork of small bones like chain mail, armored plating, tougher than leather, nature's Kevlar.

I keep on staring, hypnotized, as the face swims closer, and I hear the click of talons like curved daggers on the padded paws, and I smell carrion, while, dancing above it all, hovers a winking will-o'-the-wisp, the dim red light of the LED.

The tongue flicks again. It touches my face, a killer's kiss.

As in a fairy tale, it's the kiss that breaks the spell.

I jump back, dying a little when my leg cries out, and I keep retreating until I feel pipes behind me. I'm almost against the wall.

The creature takes his time closing in again. He knows I have nowhere to go. He lumbers lazily, his walk a shambling splay-footed strut.

My hands explore the conduits at my back. One of them is warm to the touch. Another steam pipe. Copper tubing—two lengths of it—jammed together end-to-end by a coupler bolted to the wall.

The steam, the coupler—it gives me an idea.

In a second I have the belt off again. I whip it twice at Draco, knowing I can't hold him off for long, just giving the creature's small brain something to think about.

Then I loop the belt around the pipe just ahead of the coupler, slipping it between the tubing and the wall. I cinch it tight.

The other end is wrapped around my fists. I brace a foot against the wall—and pull.

It's amazing the strength a man can find when a prehistoric animal has savaged his flesh and is poised to finish him off. And it helps that the pipe is old, the copper corroded after decades of hard use. The coupler stays put, as I expected, but the pipe on my side shudders, puts up a last show of resistance, and then surrenders as I wrench it loose.

Free of the coupler, the pipe bends with surprising ease, swinging outward, ejecting a continuous blast of superheated air.

At an angle of about forty-five degrees from the wall, the pipe stops bending. Steam continues to pour out in a rush. The dragon flinches, hissing, and the steam hisses back, and for a moment the creature is stymied, perplexed by this new enemy.

But not for long. He sidesteps the steam and comes at me again. I duck below the bent pipe and stay near the opening, shying clear of the steam. The animal hesitates, unsure what to do. I'm almost within reach, but he doesn't understand the hot, noisy stuff spewing from the uncoupled pipe.

I can't hold him off forever. He'll work up his courage eventually. I unhook the belt from the pipe and snap it at him, trying to goad him closer to the open vent. He's not buying it. He has learned that the belt can't hurt him badly. He placidly accepts a few lashes across the snout.

In an explosive burst he advances on me, crossing under the pipe, while I retreat to the other side. He swings his long body against the wall. The tail is curled behind him, threatening to strike, and the big jaws wear a bloody leer.

We've reversed positions, but it hasn't helped me. If I run, he'll give chase. If I stay put, he'll continue playing with me, feinting and parrying, driving me a few steps in one direction or another, until I make some small mistake and he brings me down.

He'll never quit. He's tasted blood.

Blood ...

My hand goes to the tourniquet, hanging limply around my ankle, a blood-soaked rag. I strip it off.

On the ladder, he went for the wound in my leg. It's the blood that attracts him. It's blood that makes him wild.

I wave the cloth like a soiled red flag, and the dragon lurches forward, snapping at air.

He wants blood. It's all he wants. The only thought in his lizard brain.

Again I taunt him with the rag. He closes with me, biting furiously, missing his target as I retract it just in time.

I'm right alongside the open end of the pipe now. I can feel the steam's hot breath.

One more flourish of the tourniquet. The dragon scampers close, and I drape the rag over the end of the pipe and jump back.

If the creature is smart, he will forget the cloth and go for me. I'm betting he's not smart. I'm betting instinct impels him to follow the scent of blood.

He doesn't hesitate. He's up on his hind legs, one foreclaw wrapped around the bent pipe, as he whips his head forward and bites down on the cloth.

On the cloth—and the spray of steam beneath it.

Before he can react, I throw the belt around his jaws and pull it tight, clamping them together, forcing his teeth to remain locked on the tube.

The steam keeps pouring out, but not into the air. Into the dragon's mouth.

He tries to twist free of the pipe, but I'm not

giving him any slack. His front claws slap frantically at the belt, at my hands. Lacerations erupt on my knuckles and fingers, but I hold on, even as the belt begins to tear.

Then something whips me from behind, something as stiff and heavy as a club. It's the tail, which I've forgotten—the tail, uncoiled and striking with full force.

I'm thrown to the floor. When I look up, I can see the dragon a yard away in the faint sputtering light from the nik-nik bag. He's ripped the belt to pieces and wrested his head free of the pipe.

He turns to me, the huge head with those small eyes, only a step or two from me. I can't get up. I lack the strength. Anyway, there's no place to go.

Draco opens his mouth, and I catch a dim, sickening glimpse of blistered flesh, a deep tunnel of wounds. The creature releases a long, angry hiss.

And he sinks down and lies still.

Dead, I think.

Dead.

I can't be sure. But he's not moving. The internal injuries he suffered must have proved too much for him. His heart gave out, maybe.

The eyes are closed. I see no sign of breath.

I dare to crawl a little closer, and with a tentative hand I feel the scaly hide.

If life is here, I can't find it.

My vision shifts its focus. In the guttering light of my improvised lantern, I raise my head to look at the camera strapped to the creature's head. I know they're watching me—Uday, Qusay, and Scar—and I know they're not laughing anymore.

"I've slain your dragon, assholes!"
My shout stirs up a storm of echoes.
The LED blinks twice more, then goes dark.
Show's over.

13

I FEEL LIKE DOING a jig, but my injured leg won't play along. Kneeling, I finger the damage. The knife wound delivered by Qusay has opened up in a long, ragged gash. Skin hangs in tatters, slippery with blood. The long daggerlike fangs tore up skin and muscle with the vicious efficiency of a threshing machine.

It's the kind of wound that requires around fifty stitches. But I won't be getting any stitches. I won't make it that long.

Remember the Komodo's secret weapon? An anticoagulant secreted by glands under the tongue, injected into a bite to prevent the blood from clotting. That stuff is circulating in my system now like a dose of rat poison. I'm bleeding out, and there's not a goddamn thing I can do about it.

I tear off my other sleeve and tie a new tourniquet, but it's strictly a stopgap measure. Without medical attention, I'm done. And I won't be seeing any doctors until I get off this Army base, which will take too damn long.

I suppose if I could climb the ladder, I might make it out in time. But that's not going to happen. I can barely stand on this leg. Even if I could mount a few rungs, I lack the strength to shove the manhole lid aside. Besides having no strength in my injured leg, I have a pair of hands that have been lacerated almost to the bone. My fingers work, but I won't be doing any bench presses.

Limping, I return to the bent pipe, still clouding this part of the tunnel with steam. My belt has been shredded, but caught in the jagged clumps of leather I find a smooth, sharp curve of bone. One of the dragon's talons, black as onyx, became entangled in the belt and was ripped free by the creature's own thrashing.

I slip it into my pocket. By now the nik-nik bag has just about burned itself out. Darkness is settling around me. I'll probably die in the dark. The prospect doesn't disturb me. I've lived most of my life in darkness. I can die in it quite comfortably.

But *they'll* die first.

I can hear them coming, by the way. I've been hearing them for the past couple of minutes. They're not being quiet about it. On the contrary, they're clomping along like a team of Clydesdales, though I doubt they're hauling any suds.

They'll have no trouble finding me. They must have a pretty good fix on my position from the video they watched. Maybe the damn camera even transmits a GPS signal; I don't know. In any case, they can follow my spoor—the blood trail and boot prints, the discarded coat and strewn ashes.

I need to even the odds as much as possible. That means getting my adversaries to divide their forces. I can't count on finding another intersecting passageway up ahead—not soon enough, anyway—but I know there's one close behind me.

Retracing my steps, I reach the bend in the tunnel with its Dantesque injunction. ABBANDEN HOPE, remember? This time I go down the alternate passage, taking the road less traveled, leaving what I hope are obvious marks. After a hundred yards, I double back, sticking close to the wall and doing my best not to disturb the tracks in the center of the walkway.

By the time I return to the intersection, my friends are close. I can see faint bluish glows flitting in the blackness like St. Elmo's fire. They're using headlamps, not night-vision gear.

They can't see me yet—I'm outside the reach of their beams, and the dying glow from the nik-nik bag is too dim to be visible at a distance—but they know I'm near.

"Hey, asshole ..." Qusay's voice, raised in a childish singsong. "Where are you ...?"

"We're coming for you, Galahad," Uday yells. "You're fucked. *Fucked!*"

Both shouts echoing madly.

Two voices. Two headlamps. Scar isn't with them.

I'm surprised she would miss out on the fun. But maybe she's not as tough as she likes to appear. Maybe she can watch death from a distance, but participation up close is a different story.

Or maybe they have only two headlamps. Yeah, that's probably it.

My fuel has given out by now. I toss the bag aside. I'm heading back in darkness to the vicinity of the broken pipe and the vanquished dragon, when a slow comber of dizziness rolls over me, nearly dropping me to my knees.

I've lost a lot of blood, and I'm going to keep on losing it. Before long, my system will start shutting down.

It's just a question of holding myself together a little longer.

Idealists say love is more powerful than hate, but hate is what's always kept me going. It keeps me going now. I want to kill these shitheads. I want to cut them, choke them, watch them die. The way they hoped to watch me.

I reach the dragon, almost slipping on a slimy puddle of saliva by his open mouth. Steam, invisible in the darkness, continues pouring from the pipe, raising the heat and humidity around me to unbearable levels. The air is impossibly thick and wet. Moving through it is like fighting through yards of damp cloth.

Here is where I'll make my stand.

Uday and Qusay have one big advantage over me. They can see in the dark, and I can't. If one of them pinpoints me in a headlamp beam, I'll be cornered, helpless.

The steam helps neutralize that advantage. It's a heavy fog that obscures everything. It's hot enough to make the eyes sting and water. Anyone hunting me here will be half-blinded by his own tears, hampered by a wall of white vapor that reflects and refracts his light.

There's another good thing about this spot. Here there be dragons—or one dragon, anyway. And either one of the bros may be tempted to take a last look at their expensive pet.

"He went this way." Uday's voice. "We saw him turn right."

They've reached the intersection.

"So why are these tracks going left?" That's Qusay.

My false trail.

"Shit." Uday again. "Maybe the fucker doubled back already."

"Or maybe it's a trick. He's smart, this asshole."

"Yeah. He's smart."

I appreciate the compliment.

There's a beat of puzzled silence as the two masterminds try to reason out their next move. Uday is first to supply an answer.

"We'll split up. You go to the left. I'll go right."

Uday will be coming for me, then. That's good. For some reason I dislike him more than his brother. Because he's such a big talker, I guess.

I retreat to the ladder under the manhole. I can't climb it, but I can use it for cover. Crouching behind it, making myself as small as possible, hidden by the dragon's inert mass and by drifts of steam, I just may avoid being spotted.

What will happen from this point forward is mainly about luck. I don't kid myself about that. Uday has a gun and a light source. I don't even have a belt anymore. If he sees me squatting here, he'll finish me off with a single trigger pull. There's nothing I can do about that.

But it may not play out that way.

Footsteps. A distant, diffuse, traveling glow. He's coming.

I can't see him from where I'm hidden. But

through a scrim of steam I see the tunnel walls brighten as the headlamp draws near. In the artificial light, the steam looks ghostly, an ectoplasmic cloud.

Spirits of the dead. The men who've died in these tunnels ... a dozen of them ... phantoms, wraiths lost in the depths of Sheol ...

Quit that.

I need to maintain concentration. The next half minute will decide things.

The beam swings down in time with the movement of Uday's head as he registers the carcass at his feet. Right now he's standing at an angle to my hiding place. He could see me if he were to turn his head just a little. But for the moment, he's distracted.

The headlamp beam wavers, panning the dragon's body, flickering from the long, stiffly curled tail to the splayed hind legs, then to the barrel-shaped belly and the big foreclaws, and finally along the wrinkled dewlap to the great, greasy jaws crowded with teeth and blood and drool, and, looming above them, one dead black eye nested in furrows of leathery hide.

And the camera, still perched like a crown on the grinning inhuman head.

Uday hesitates. Then with decision he steps closer, reaching for the camera. He wants to salvage it.

His back is turned to me. I'll never have a better chance.

You can't be a professional killer if you're either clumsy or slow. I've never been either. Even now, half-dead and bleeding out, I'm on my feet and closing the distance between us in less time than it takes to draw a breath.

Instinct. Reflex. Muscle memory. My body still functional, against all logic and all odds. I move with practiced slip-sliding steps, making no noise.

At the last instant Uday starts to turn. I've done nothing to give myself away. It's just the sixth sense we all have, the instinctive alertness of a stag at a watering hole.

But it comes too late.

I seize his face with one hand, cupping his nose and mouth with my fingers, and with the other hand I spike the dragon's talon deep into his throat. Then with a smooth twist of my arm I inscribe a semicircular gash below his chin from ear to ear.

He doesn't scream. He lost that opportunity when the claw punched through his windpipe. He makes low, frantic choking noises, a man drowning in his own blood.

Noises I've heard many times before. The soundtrack of my life.

His gun goes off.

He hasn't fired at me. It's only a spasm of his forefinger. The single round strikes metal somewhere with a reverberating ping.

Before he can shoot again, I snatch the pistol out of his hand. When I let go of him, he falls on his knees by the dragon, as if prostrating himself before a dark idol. His hands come up—another dying reflex, but it looks like a gesture of supplication. For a long moment, he kneels with arms upraised, until he bends at the waist and falls forward onto the dragon's belly, burying his face in its hide.

My head is swimming. The intense heat and the steam, the physical effort and the blood loss—it's all taking its toll.

But I'm not done yet.

"Jalal?"

Qusay's shout, excited, happy.

"Jalal, did you get him? Did you get him?"

So the late Uday was actually Jalal. Distantly I find this interesting. I always like knowing someone's name.

With shaking fingers, I pull the headlamp off Uday's corpse and snag it crookedly on my forehead. The beam is powerful enough to wash out the figure behind it. To Qusay I'll be only a haloed shadow in a blurred steam bath.

A bright cyclopean eye appears at the far end of the tunnel, expanding in a tattoo of racing footfalls.

"You get him, bro?"

I lift the gun and fire three times at a point below Qusay's headlamp, aiming for the spot where neck meets breastbone.

This, too, is something I've done before. Many times.

The headlamp spins and hits the floor. I fire twice more into the center mass of a twitching human form until it lies still.

Then I sag, supporting myself against the wall, feeling energy and willpower drain out of me along with my lifeblood.

I've done it. Killed the pair of them. I can rest now. Rest ...

Except I can't.

Because of Scar.

She wasn't a member of the shooting party. But that doesn't mean she gets a pass.

14

WITH SLOW STUMBLING STEPS, I approach Qusay. I turn him onto his back. At close range my headlamp washes out his features like an overexposed portrait. I see the beginnings of mustache stubble above his upper lip. I see his eyes staring without sight, his nostrils dilated, his mouth open. He looks surprised. People so often do when they get shot.

I leave him there and proceed along the corridor the way I came.

Moving slowly, but moving. That's the important thing.

My torn-up leg hurts like a bastard. But the pain, though real, seems strangely impersonal. Someone else's problem.

Put one foot in front of the other ... one foot in front of the other ...

I'm not so much walking as shuffling. When I look back, the beam from my forehead shows me a long, smeared snail trail of blood.

How much blood is in the human body, anyway? That's one of those trivia items I ought to know. I think I do know it. Or I did. Seem to have forgotten now. Hard to focus. Hard to remember anything.

Except Rebecca. She's the one thing I can't forget.

I've tried often enough. I've wished her away. I've cursed her name. I've ordered her to leave me alone. Bitch doesn't listen. Bitch is always here. Is here now.

Staring at me. Staring with wide, frightened eyes.

I was looking into those eyes when I pulled the trigger and put a hole in her left cheek, a perfect round entry wound that dropped her to the floor of Alex Dura's kitchen.

She was with him that night. I didn't know. How could I? Julie never let me be part of the girl's life. Never let me see her. I knew nothing about my own daughter. Not even what she looked like as a young woman, nineteen years old.

As it turned out, Julie didn't know a whole hell of a lot more than I did. She believed she'd kept Rebecca safe. She believed the girl was uncontaminated by exposure to the dangerous people her mother knew.

But Scar was right about that much. Kids always find out what their parents are up to. Rebecca must have eavesdropped on enough conversations to get the drift. And naturally she wanted to taste that forbidden life for herself.

I don't know how she met up with Dura. Through Julie, obviously, but the details are purely speculative. Maybe she followed Julie to work and saw him come out of the office. Maybe Dura showed up at the house some night, running an errand for his boss. Who knows?

Dura was young, charming, good looking enough.

And by all accounts, a big talker. I hate big talkers. He must have talked her pants off...

Literally, I mean. I guess that's a joke. Not sure. Can't tell. My sense of humor seems to be bleeding out along with everything else.

Anyway, she started seeing him. I didn't know. *I did not know.* I thought Dura was alone. I killed him in his bed. I was leaving when the girl stepped out of the kitchen, a glass of water in her hand.

A stranger to me. Just some whore. Alex Dura's squeeze. Looking at me.

The hitman's credo: *No witnesses.*

I didn't even have to think about it. I shot her, and she fell backward onto the tiled floor, the water glass spilling its contents without breaking. I spared a moment to confirm she was dead. The eyes were frozen, unblinking. She looked surprised. I'm telling you, it's amazing how often they look like that. As if death is some kind of novelty. As if they—we—shouldn't be expecting it all the time, at any moment.

I left Dura's apartment. I went home. I showered. I slept. I had no dreams. I never dreamed back then.

It was two days later when I saw it in the paper. Local paper, delivered to my door. Small story on an inside page. The names of the victims. Dura, of course.

And Rebecca. Her name, rendered in blunt typeface on the cheap newsprint.

I read this, and read it again. I may have read a dozen times. Then I went into the bathroom. I shaved. I patted my face. I looked at the man in the mirror. He looked back.

And that was the end of my old life. The end of me, or of any part of me that matters.

She's been with me ever since. Rebecca. Haunting me. She's in my head. In my dreams. I hoped I could exorcise her by saving the red-haired girl in the luxury car. Balance the scales or something.

But the scales never balance. Not for a man like me.

By now I'm lurching drunkenly along one wall, hugging the pipes to stay upright. One of the pipes scalds my hand. It's the one I used to melt off the handcuffs. Below it, I see the neatly folded oilskin duster.

I stoop. I put it on. This takes effort. Wears me out. But I need the coat. I'm feeling cold. Here, in this tropical sweatbox—cold.

Another swooning sensation threatens to overtake me. I brace my hands on my knees, head lowered, the headlamp washing me in its cold electric glare, until the worst passes.

Standing there, marshaling my last reserves of strength, I hear a noise.

A faint noise, but familiar.

Against all reason, I feel my lips bend into a smile.

15

TIME PASSES, MEASURED IN yard after yard after yard. Flat concrete sliding like a long gray ribbon under my boots. I feel no pain anymore. I feel nothing. I may be dead already. Dead man walking.

It's all right. I've been that way for the last six years. Only now, the skull beneath the skin is grinning a little more fiercely than before.

Coming to join you, Rebecca, I think. But I don't believe it. I'm not joining anyone. I'll wink out like a snuffed match. Like she did. Like we all do. Gone. Just gone.

Step after step after step, and finally there it is, emerging from the gloom into the nebulous circle of my headlamp beam. The staircase leading to the office where they screened the video for me—Uday and Qusay and Scar.

Two of them dead now. The third waiting her turn.

The stairs intimidate me. Climbing them seems as unthinkable as climbing the endless laddered tiers of a ziggurat. Ziggurat, what a word. Wonder where I picked up that one. Some show about Babylon. Monument builders, tomb builders, Tower of Babel, God sowing confusion among the nations, confused language, confused thought ...

Focus. Climb.

Up I go. I cling to the metal railing. Lifting my legs is an exercise in torture. But I'm doing it. Where there's a will, there's a way. Right, Mom?

At the top now. The landing. Cooler here. Cold, in fact. Ice cold. Or is that me?

The door hanging ajar. Unlocked. That's good. It would be awkward to ask Scar to open it.

I pull it toward me. It seems impossibly heavy. Everything is heavy. The air itself is dense like water.

When the door is half-open, I go inside. As before, the room is lit only by the computer screen. Scar lounges at the card table, idly fingering the trackpad. She throws a casual glance at the doorway.

"I hope you made him suffer," she says. "I loved that fucking lizard."

She isn't seeing me, only a headlamp in the dark.

My lips move. I feel suddenly stronger. Alive, almost.

"You've never loved anything, Scar."

I give her credit for the speed of her reaction. She bolts from her chair and has her gun half out of her purse before I shoot her.

Not fatally, though. I've missed the heart.

Intentionally.

She hits the floor, losing the gun. She scrabbles for it with one clutching hand. Captured in the beam of light, that hand looks like a pale, fleshy spider crawling raggedly across the floor.

I cross the room, kick the gun out of her reach, take her by the hair—her long red hair, a fairy-tale princess's hair—and I drag her to the open door and through it, onto the landing. The light from my headlamp bounces everywhere, fracturing off the railing beside me and the pipes below.

She's twisting, struggling. Even wounded, she ought to be able to overpower me in my present condition. Somehow I'm more than her equal. Because of hate. Hate, my old friend, my constant companion. Hate, which makes me strong.

"I came here," I tell her gravely, "to do two things. Save the maiden and slay the dragon."

"Let me go," she moans.

"Two things, Scar." I lower my head, and the beam washes over the floor at the foot of the staircase. "And I didn't do either."

The floor lights up. In the glow, a long reptilian form lies waiting.

That's when Scar begins to scream.

"No, no, *no!*"

As an argument, it isn't very persuasive.

I thought I'd killed Draco. But while he was down, he wasn't out. He was stunned, immobilized. After a time, he recovered. And he came after me.

It was when I collected my coat that I heard the click-clack of his nails on the floor. That familiar sound.

And I was glad.

I can't hate Draco. It's not his fault he's trapped down here, chasing human vermin for the entertainment of sick clowns with nothing better to do. He's as much a victim in this as I am.

And even after what he's done to me, I have no wish to dispatch him. I guess I've decided to take a pass on sainthood.

So I didn't use Uday's gun on him. I just kept walking. I could hear him behind me, dogging my steps, but keeping a wary distance. By now we respect each other, you see. I hurt him, and he hurt me. He isn't going to do anything rash. He will simply follow and await his opportunity. Why not? He knows he cut me. He knows I'll bleed out soon.

In the meantime, though, he really should eat something.

Still holding Scar by the hair, I hoist her half-upright against the tubular rail.

In the old days, they sacrificed virgins to dragons. I'm guessing Scarlett LeShawn is no virgin.

But she'll have to do.

I shove her forward, over the railing, into space. There's nothing to break her fall until she lands on the hard concrete ten feet down.

If she were lucky, she'd have broken her neck. She isn't lucky. It's her legs that are broken—both of them, if I can judge by the way they're twisted at unnatural angles.

"You piece of shit!" Her words come out in explosive gasps. "Piece of *shit!*"

A yard away, Draco stirs.

"Shade, God damn you. God fucking damn you, Shade!"

"My name's not Shade," I say.

Scar tries to stand, can't. She drags herself to the bottom of the staircase, hauling her useless legs behind her, and clutches madly at the railing, but her grip is weak and sweaty and she slips free.

And the dragon uncurls with slow majesty and a disdainful flick of its tongue.

Scar screams again. She's smelled its breath, I think. That carrion smell, like roadkill.

She grabs the railing again, and this time she's able to pull herself onto the steps, clambering upward, struggling to reach the imagined safety of higher ground.

Draco is in no hurry. There's something magnificent in his indifference, something regal, lordly. With slow deliberation he places one front foot —a foot that's missing a talon—on the lowest step. His long tongue extends to lick her leg. The wide, bloody mouth splits in a gaping leer.

Scar stares up at me, her face wild.

"It's not fair! *It's not fair!*"

I have no opinion about this. Justice is something I long ago ceased to expect.

But I think the man in the video, the one who did the paindance, would have found it fair.

Straining at the railing, she hauls her body up one more step.

And Draco lunges.

The jaws seize her left leg and twist it viciously. Bone explodes through the skin. Scar releases a strangled cry more eloquent than any howl of pain. She sinks back, stunned into acquiescence, and the dragon releases the leg and scissors open her midsection.

Standard predator behavior. The viscera, the easiest parts of the carcass to ingest, are usually claimed first.

I have no desire to watch what follows. Unlike Scar and her friends, I'm no connoisseur of pain.

The office is just behind me. Beyond it is the

parking lot, the night sky, the cool air. I can go outside now.

But I won't. Here is where I belong, here in these concrete catacombs.

When I'm sure the dragon is fully preoccupied with his meal, I go down the stairs, stepping boldly past him. I mean to continue my tour of Hades. And perhaps after I'm dead, Draco will find me and feed. The idea pleases me. One warrior feasting on the corpse of another.

Scar, by the way, is still alive. As I pass her, I see her face jerking with tics of amazed pain as Draco unwinds the intestines from her belly and slurps them down.

I avert my gaze and move on, content to let the spectacle proceed without me. I head off into the tunnels and leave the ugly smacking and crunching noises behind.

At a certain point I toss away Uday's gun and then his headlamp. I walk on in darkness. My last flare-up of strength is already ebbing. Blood loss, mounting. Crazy thoughts afloat in my brain. Images in the darkness. Men I killed. They all look surprised. Rebecca. Her staring eyes.

Walking the maze of tunnels. Traveling along corridors of darkness, down side passageways, doubling back when I hit a dead end. Walking until I've lost my way in the labyrinth.

My head is hollow, airy. I hear a high tinkling sound, like wind chimes.

The man in the mirror. Have I outrun him yet? No, he's still with me.

But he doesn't scare me anymore.

I wonder when they'll find me here, and how much will be left to find. I carry no ID. I'll be just another unknown victim, to be interred in an unmarked grave. That's okay. I don't like people knowing my name.

My strongest desire is to stop walking. To lower myself to the floor. Rest my head against the wall. Let my eyes close. Sleep.

I go on. I will not sleep. I've been asleep most of my life, asleep and dreaming terrible dreams. I was asleep when I shot Rebecca. I was asleep until I saw the man in the mirror. That man was my wake-up call. I must be true to him.

No rest for me, Not while I breathe. I'll keep going until the last of my heart's blood is gone.

I've lived as a sleepwalker.

But I'll die wide awake.

AUTHOR'S NOTE

READERS ARE INVITED TO visit my author website, michaelprescott.net, where you can find links to all my books, news about upcoming projects, contact info, and other stuff.

The idea for *Die Wide Awake* came to me when Google celebrated the thirty-seventh anniversary of Komodo National park with a doodle of a dragon lizard. For some reason, the accompanying info on these creatures made me wonder what would happen if some sickos decided to keep one in the hot, humid environment of a steam-tunnel system, where it could be used for blood sport. I doubt Google had this particular scenario in mind when they came up with the doodle.

As always, thanks to Diana Cox of www.novel-proofreading.com for a meticulous proofreading job. And thanks to all you good folks who keep buying—and reading—my books!

—MP

ABOUT THE AUTHOR

After twenty years in traditional publishing, Michael Prescott found himself unable to sell another book. On a whim, he began releasing his novels in digital form. Sales took off, and by 2011 he was one of the world's best-selling e-book writers.

Made in the USA
Monee, IL
31 January 2021